ONCE UPON A MORE
ENLIGHTENED TIME

ONCE UPON A MORE ENLIGHTENED TIME

More Politically Correct Bedtime Stories

JAMES FINN GARNER

MACMILLAN • USA

MACMILLAN
A Simon & Schuster Macmillan Company
15 Columbus Circle
New York, NY 10023

Library of Congress Cataloging-in-Publication Data available

ISBN 0-02-860419-9

Manufactured in the United States of America
10 9 8 7 6 5 4 3 2 1

Dedicated to Anne Conrad-Antoville, principal cellist with the Eureka (California) Symphony Orchestra, who chose compassion over culture by resigning her position rather than perform "Peter and the Wolf," an orchestral work that teaches our pre-adults to fear and despise wolves and other wild predators.

Also, and more importantly, to Lies and Nyuji.

CONTENTS

INTRODUCTION

At the outset, I would like to apologize sincerely for the success of my last book. The number of trees that voicelessly gave their lives so that my resource-greedy publisher and I could meet retail demand was truly appalling, and quite likely contributed to the global warming that gave those of us in the Northern Hemisphere such an unseasonably warm winter. We have made every effort to make this second volume more Earth-friendly, using natural soy inks, people-powered bicycle delivery systems, and photo-degradable paper that will revert to its basic organic components within a short time if exposed to light or read in the tub.

Next, I would like to apologize for exposing myself in my last book to be such an etymo-patriarchalist. As an alert reader in The Netherlands pointed out, while I used the proper spelling of the word "wommon" throughout *Politically Correct Bedtime Stories*, I still swaggered around, waving my phallocentric spellings of "person" and "human" in everyone's face. Properly penitent, in this volume I have opted to use the inclusive, gender-neutral spelling "persun." Unfortunately, a cultural-linguistic Catch-22 prevents me from using "hummon" or "hummun" because both spellings are rather nasty epithets in certain dialects spoken throughout the islands of Micronesia. Therefore, rather than offend those oft-oppressed and exploited peoples if and when this book is ever distributed in their region, I regretfully must choose to offend instead the oppressors and exploiters of the English-speaking world (you know who you are).

You hold in your hands another flawed yet earnest attempt to purge the "children's" stories popular in "Western" "culture" from the biases and prejudices that ran unchecked in their original "versions." Stretching as far back as Aesop and the Greco-Roman patriarchy he represents, I have chosen from a wide range of narratives based on familiarity and copyright protection. Sadly, space restrictions have forced us once again to omit "The Duckling that Was Judged on Its Persunal Merits and Not on Its Physical Appearance." I heartily apologize to all proponents of young waterfowl literature; please do not write or E-mail.

Once again, if through omission or commission I have inadvertently displayed any racist, sexist, cultural-ist, speciesist, socio-economicist, or other type of bias (including ism-ist divisiveness), I deeply apologize and stand open to correction. I am not and never claimed to be an expert, merely a citizen concerned with the effect of literature on our younger persuns. That I choose to use a book as the means to combat these influences may be ironic (irony itself being one of many suspect attitudes imported from the literary world), but it is the best effort I can muster at this stage of my persunal evolution. If this bibliocentric decision in any way offends, I ask you to find it in your heart, my enlightened reader, to forgive me.

A POLITICALLY CORRECT ALPHABET*

A is an **A**ctivist itching to fight.

B is a **B**east with its animal rights.

C was a **C**ripple (now differently abled).

D is a **D**runk who is "liquor-enabled."

E is an **E**cologist who saves spotted owls.

F was a **F**orester, now staffing McDonald's.

G is a **G**lutton who says he's "food-centered."

H is a **H**ermaphrodite skirting problems of gender.

I is an "**I**sm" (you'd better believe it).

J is a **J**ingoist—love it or leave it!

K is a **K**ettle the pot can't call black.

L is a **L**ifestyle not bound to the pack.

M is a **M**indset with bias galore.

N was a **N**egro, but not anymore.

O is an **O**ppressor, devoid of self-love.

P is the **P**atriarchy (see "O" above).

Q is a **Q**uip that costs someone a job.

R is the **R**easoning done by a mob.

S is a **S**exist, that slobbering menace.

T is a **T**eapot that's brewing a tempest.

U is for **U**mbrage at the slightest transgression.

V is a **V**alentine, tool of oppression.

W is for "**W**oman," however it's spelled.

X is a chromosome we share in our cells.

Y is a **Y**ogi for the easily led.

Z is a **Z**ombie, the differently dead.

* The traditional order of the letters in an alphabet is, of course, completely arbitrary. In spite of its association with excellence in archaic, competitive, literacy-obsessed school grading programs, A is no better or more deserving a letter than X, Y, or Z.

Therefore, to deflect any criticisms of a noun-centric bias, I employed a random-letter generator before working on this new alphabet. Believe me, I was as surprised as anyone that, despite the tremendous odds, the random-letter generator spat out the alphabet in the exact order shown above.

HANSEL AND GRETEL

eep in a forested bioregion stood a small, humble chalet, and in that chalet lived a small, humble family. The father was a tree butcher by trade, and he was doing his best to raise his two pre-adults named Hansel and Gretel.

The family tried to maintain a healthy and conscientious lifestyle, but the demands of the capitalist system, especially its irresponsible energy policies, worked ceaselessly to smother them. Soon they were at a complete economic disadvantage and found themselves unable to live in the style to which they had become accustomed, paltry though it may have been. With the little money that was coming in, there was not enough to feed them all.

So, regretfully, the tree butcher was forced to devise a plan to be rid of his children. He decided to take them deep into the woods as he went about his daily work and then abandon them there. It was a sad commentary on the plight of single-parent households, but he could see no alternative.

When the father discussed this plan on the phone with his analyst, Hansel overheard the conversation. Instead of alerting the proper authorities, Hansel came up with a plan for protecting himself and his sibling. The next morning, the tree butcher packed them all sensible, nutritious lunches in reusable containers and they set off. Hansel, however, had filled his pockets with granola, and as they walked deeper and deeper into the woods, he dropped large chunks of it on the path to mark the way.

At a clearing deep in the woods, the tree butcher finally stopped and said to Hansel and Gretel, "You pre-adults wait here. I'm going to look for some trees to harvest, and maybe explore my primitive masculine psyche against the backdrop of nature, if I have time. I'll be back before too long." He handed the children their lunches and walked off.

After morning had turned into afternoon and afternoon into evening, Hansel told his sister their father's plan to abandon them. Gretel, always level-headed and practical in such situations, suggested they collect materials for a lean-to shelter, as they'd learned in their Outward Bound Aboriginal Survival Techniques class.

"No need," said Hansel. "I've left us a trail to follow back, without even littering or defacing a single tree." But when they went to find the trail, they discovered a cadre of survivalists busily eating up the granola. The survivalists screamed at the children to get away from their newfound rations and, after firing a few warning shots in the air, disappeared into the woods.

Hansel and Gretel wandered along different trails, but after some time they became hopelessly lost and very hungry. Then, around a sharp bend in their path, they came upon a wondrous cottage made of carob brownies, sugarless gingerbread, and carrot cake. Even without a reassuring FDA label, the cottage looked so good that the children dived at it and began to devour it.

Suddenly, a wommon in her golden years (actually, quite past them) emerged from the cottage. The many bangles on her wrists and ankles clattered as she moved, and she gave off the aroma of patchouli, burnt sage, and clove cigarettes. The children were startled. Hansel asked, "Please forgive my bluntness, but are you a wicked witch?"

The wommon laughed. "No, no, my dear. I'm not a witch, I'm a Wiccan. I'm no more evil than anyone else, and I certainly don't eat little pre-adults, like all the rumors would have you believe. I worship nature and the Goddess, and mix herbs and natural potions to help people. Really. Now why don't you both come in for a nice cup of coltsfoot tea?"

Inside the functional yet edible cottage, the Wiccan advised the children to forget the propaganda and slander that had been spread about persuns like her. She told them stories about her life in the forest, making potions, casting spells, communing with non-human animals, and healing the many wounds inflicted on Mother Earth. It took some time for Hansel and Gretel to free their minds from the stereotype of a green-skinned, temporally advanced crone in a pointy black hat. (Ironically, the Wiccan did have a long warty nose that resembled a moldy cucumber, but the children were too polite to ask about it.)

They were finally convinced of the Wiccan's sincerity when they met her neighbors and kinsfolk. To welcome the children, these gentle people held a gathering that night in the moonlight, in which they stripped off all their clothes, rubbed mud on each other, and danced in a circle to the sound of ocarinas and panpipes. It was an inspiring sight, and it felt so right and natural that Hansel and Gretel decided then and there to give up their old lives and join the forest people.

Over time, Hansel and Gretel came to love the Wiccan and their lives in the forest. As they grew older and more empowered, they began to assert their bonds with Mother Earth in more direct and tangible ways. With courage and vigor, they planned and engaged in many deep ecology actions to protect their arboreal home. Hansel and Gretel merrily spiked trees, monkey-wrenched mining and bull-dozing equipment, and blew up power plants and electrical lines that stretched over nearby farmland with explosives made from all-natural ingredients. They even learned 15 completely organic remedies for powder burns.

They were very content and self-fulfilled protect-ing their adopted habitat until one day terrible news came. A huge multinational paper conglomerate had purchased their entire forest, intent on turning it all into wood pulp. Hansel, Gretel, the Wiccan, and all their compadres and com-madres geared up for the confrontation of their lives. The eco-defenders gathered up their wrenches and their plastique, their picket signs and their panpipes, and started off for the headquarters of the conglomerate, alerting the media along the way that they were ready to defend Our Mother to the very last persun.

Hansel, Gretel, and the Wiccan marched at the head of the crowd, chanting and swaying and itching for a fight. As the headquarters of the paper company came into view, the two siblings saw something about it that was very familiar. The huge plant and building complex took up nearly four acres of land, but on the circular driveway, smack in the middle of the main entrance, sat a small, humble chalet. It was in fact their childhood home, squatting like a hermit's shack in front of the sleek steel and glass facade of the HQ.

Just as the brother and sister were beginning to digest this, the small wooden door of the shack opened and out stepped their father, the tree butcher. He was dressed in an Armani suit with Italian loafers, and on either side of him crowded a phalanx of lawyers. It was obvious that the woodspersun had done OK for himself.

"Well, well," said the father, "the wheel of fate spins round again. Good to see you again, Hansel and Gretel."

"Please, don't call us that," said his biological but not spiritual son. "We have changed our names to symbolize the birth of our new consciousness and to separate ourselves from our heartless, exploitative upbringing. From now on, you may call me Heathdweller."

"And my name is Gaia," said his sister.

"Change your names to Thumper and Bambi, for all I care," their father laughed. "You people are still going to have to relocate from the forest. We've made a deal with a nice trailer park down by the Interstate for you, and hired a relocation counseling firm to help—"

The Wiccan cut him off. "Death to the rapers of Earth! Death to the rapers of Earth!" she screamed, and the rest of the crowd picked up her chant.

"No need to get personal," the father muttered. He moved to calm the crowd. "All right, all right. We'd like to meet with your spokesman—"

"Spokeswommon!" insisted one protester.

"Spokespersun!" shouted another.

A lawyer whispered into the father's ear. "We'd like to meet with your persun of spoke," the father said finally, "the Wiccan."

Amid shouts of encouragement the Wiccan raised her fist and walked into the building with the suits. The ecoteurs were very happy and confident because they placed their complete trust in the Wiccan. She would never back down in the face of these planet ravishers. To celebrate, they formed a prayer circle in the parking lot and began to dance.

The sound of ocarinas and panpipes was still in the air when the negotiators reemerged from the building. The father and the lawyers were smiling, while the Wiccan had a more sheepish expression, although it is an insult to sheep to imply that they could ever look so guilty.

Gaia, née Gretel, immediately sensed that something in the established order of things had changed. "What's happened?" she insisted. "What went on in there?"

"A prominent member of your group has decided to wake up and face reality," said her father. "The Wiccan has agreed to join our senior staff, as our new Vice President of Holistic and Spiritual Wellness, Mother Earth Division."

An involuntary gasp escaped from the eco-warriors. "How could you?" screamed Gaia.

"Child, I had no choice," she said in a pleading manner. "They gave me complete medical and dental, including experimental cures that most policies won't cover."

A confused murmur went up from the eco-squadron. This was indeed a stunning blow. If their wisest and most earth-conscious persun-in-arms could be so easily bought, what chance did the rest of them have? Along with the lawyers around him, the tree butcher wore a grin like the cat that had satisfied its nutritional needs at the expense of the canary.

But Hansel—oops!—Heathdweller and Gaia were well acquainted with their father's ruthlessness and had devised a back-up plan. With great pomp and flurry, they each put on hooded robes, drew a pentagram on the ground, and burned dried herbs in a small crucible. Everyone looked on in curiosity, and perhaps with a little fear. Then the brother and sister chanted an invocation in a language that even the Wiccan had never heard. The wind began to blow and the air crackled. Then, with a flash of light, it was done. The entire papermaking operation—headquarters building, plant, and warehouse complexes—had changed from steel and concrete to peppermint sticks, gingerbread, and gumdrops.

The ecoteurs' mouths hung open, then they let out a cheer. The lawyers conferred among themselves and jotted notes about possible action plans in their Filofaxes. The Wiccan just stood there while her mouth formed a silent "Wow."

The tree butcher put on a brave front. "Nice trick, kids, but you haven't stopped me. The plant is still as sturdy as ever, and now my maintenance costs are down to a little frosting and fudge. Thanks very much. We'll still keep operating, and we're still going to tear down your forest."

Heathdweller and Gaia didn't answer him, but instead burned more herbs and breathed more incantations. The wind again blew and the air crackled, and before everyone's eyes, the entire squad of lawyers was turned into a horde of mice—very *hungry* mice—who immediately swarmed over the huge, sticky-sweet industrial complex that lay before them and began to devour it.

The Wiccan had no idea that the siblings were so well versed in the black arts. She tried to appease them with flattery: "That was very impressive. We have a lot to teach each other, don't we? I'm looking forward to sharing our knowledge together in an open and supportive—" but her words were cut short as Heathdweller and Gaia flicked their paranormal whip and transformed her from a wommon in her golden years to a slinky, white-bellied weasel. The former Wiccan then ran off to join the mice in their factory feeding frenzy.

Their father was now visibly shaken as he watched the work of a lifetime being squeakily devoured. Ever the master of the guilt trip, he finally said, "And this is how you kids repay me? Do you think it was easy being a single working parent? If I hadn't brought you into the woods that day, you wouldn't have found this whole new life for yourselves. And this is the thanks I get? What about my needs? I've been in the wood business all my life, now what am I supposed to do?"

So Heathdweller and Gaia did him a favor and turned him into a beaver.

After this ordeal, the ecoheroes picked up their placards and headed back into the forest.

Heathdweller and Gaia worked hard at perfecting their supernatural skills, which they put to use solely for defending the planet. Their neighbors respected the siblings' privacy, lest a stray incantation turn them into a different (though certainly not inferior) species. And the magickal brother and sister, their friends, and, most important, the trees of the forest lived happily ever after.

THE ANT AND THE GRASSHOPPER

n the world of the ancient Greeks, agriculture was still in a state of advanced rudimentariness. The farm ecosystems were diverse and healthy, with indigenous free-range plants and thriving insect colonies sharing space with the domesticated crops. As a result, the fields of wheat and grapes were filled with a variety of vigorous, forward-looking, and well-spoken insects. The most industrious of these was the ant. All summer long he worked in the hot sun, storing away grain and seeds in anticipation of a long winter.

In that same field lived a grasshopper whose life was very free from care, since he had long ago rejected the bourgeois, money-grubbing concept of "making it." To him, the ideal existence was to enjoy Nature in an unstructured and playfully exploratory manner, and he often took advantage of His/Her/Its beneficence by sleeping most of the day. At other times, he would sing joyfully in the meadow, *churREEP churREEP*, thus keeping alive the rich oral tradition of the grasshoppers.

This alternative attitude did not go unnoticed by the ant, as he toiled in the heat and dust. When he saw the grasshopper enjoying life on his own terms, it made every orifice in his exoskeleton cinch up tight.

"Look at that grasshopper," the ant muttered to himself. "Sitting around on his abdomen all day, singing his blasted songs. When will he ever show some responsibility? To call him a leech would be an insult to all the hardworking segmented worms in this country. He's just watching me, waiting for the chance to jump me and take everything I've worked so hard for. That's the way it is with his phylum."

For his part, the grasshopper was also watching the ant, but with an entirely different train of thought.

16

"Look at that ant," he mused, "working so hard to accumulate his little store of grain. And for what? If only he would try to be a little more Zen-like. He might understand that, to the stone, one kernel of grain is the same as one thousand, and the rain never has to worry about its penmanship."

So the summer went. The ant, a quintessential type-A persunality, worked himself into a frenzy every day, but his selfish and socially irresponsible activity took its toll. He developed a peptic ulcer, had some scares with thorax pains, and lost most of the hair on the top of his head. In mid-September, his wife left him and took the pupae, but he scarcely noticed. The ant became so obsessed with his store of grain that he went so far as to install an elaborate security system in and around his anthill, with video cameras and motion sensors to catch any would-be thief.

In between naps, the grasshopper watched all this with detached curiosity. He also studied hatha yoga, scoured the area for the perfect cup of cappuccino, taught himself to play the guitar (really only one song, a self-penned, quasi-blues number with three notes), and generally hung out. He tried to keep his leisure-centric lifestyle attuned to the passing of the seasons. When the weather turned less congenial, he planned to go to Australia and do a little surfing.

But winter arrived early that year (or summer left too soon, depending on your climatic orientation) and the fields were quickly barren. The unfortunate grasshopper found himself a victim of the capriciousness of meteorological change. He went hopping about the field, looking for sustenance of any kind. He would have settled for a crumb, a husk, a bit of tofu—but nothing edible could be found.

Soon the grasshopper spotted the ant, lustily dragging a full cornstalk behind him. The grasshopper's hunger got the better of his pride, and he walked over, intending to ask the ant to share a little of his immense hoard. But as soon as he caught sight of the grasshopper, the ant began to scream.

"AAAHHHHH!!! What do you want? What are you doing here? You've come to take my cornstalk, haven't you? I know you've been plotting the day when you would snatch away everything I own! Your type are all the same!"

The grasshopper tried to interrupt, but the ant raved on: "Don't say anything! Don't try to work your wiles on me, with your sob stories and empty promises! I've worked hard for what I have, even if that might not be fashionable in some circles."

The grasshopper said politely, "But surely, Brother Ant, you have more than you could ever possibly eat."

"That's my business," said the ant, "and we don't live in some blood-sucking socialist state . . . *yet!* Get with the program, grasshopper! The only place where success comes before work is in the dictionary."

"I was planning to go to Australia, see, but the weather, like, *changed* and all the food has disappeared. . . . "

"That's how a free market works, pal. Take a lesson."

"Forgive me, Brother Ant, but I feel obliged to say, like, I think you need to work on your karma. The aura you're giving off is full of negative energy, which you could easily convert into positive by simply—"

"Look, you want to get all mystical on me, then tell me: What's the sound of one bug starving? Ha ha!"

The ant and the grasshopper were interrupted in their fruitless debate by the sound of a cough. They turned and saw a huge mantis bigger than the two of them put together! (The mantis was at one time a praying mantis but had been prohibited from such practices by court order. He did, however, retain a deeply spiritual side.) The ant and the grasshopper were frightened, not by the mantis's larger-than-proportionally-average size but by the nonsense-free aspect of his appearance. He wore a gray polyester suit and brown loafers with tassels, and in his forelegs he carried a briefcase, a brown paper lunch bag, and a calculator.

"Ant?" the mantis asked, even though he knew exactly which one he was looking for. "Ant, I've come for an audit."

With those six ominous words, the course of our story changes. Omitting the details of the audit, and the contested charges, and the suit and countersuit, and the ant's attempted flight to the Caymans, suffice it to say that the greedy insect's hoard was appropriated and put to more responsible community uses after he was enrolled in the correctional system. The grasshopper, meanwhile, organized a program for young area insects eager for cultural interchange with countries with warmer climates. Thanks to government revenue redistribution (and the ant's estate), the grasshopper has been directing surfing expeditions from that day to this.

THE PRINCESS AND THE PEA

n a kingdom over the hills and far away, there lived a young prince who was very full of himself. He was healthy, relatively handsome, and had had more than his fair share of happiness and comfort growing up. Yet he felt that he deserved something more. It was not enough for him to have been born into a life of parasitical leisure and to keep the masses firmly under the heel of his calfskin boot. He was also determined to perpetuate this undemocratic tyranny by marrying only a real, authentic, card-carrying princess.

His mother the queen encouraged her son's obsession, despite the obvious risks of hemophiliac or microcephalic grandchildren. Many years earlier, after a period of inadequate wellness, his father the king had achieved corporal terminality. This lack of a strong male presence gnawed at the prince on a sub-conscious level, and no amount of weekend retreats and male bonding with other young dukes and barons could relieve this anxiety. His mother, for her own codependent and Oedipal reasons, did not bother to change or correct his selfish notions of unattainable perfection in a spousal lifemate.

In his quest for the perfect partner, the prince travelled far and wide, looking for someone to enslave in matrimony. Astride his trusty equine colleague, he went from kingdom to queendom and from dukedom to duchessdom, asking for names and phone numbers. Heavily or lightly pigmented, vertically or horizontally challenged, cosmetically attractive or differently visaged—he cared not a whit. His only criterion was the royal authenticity of a wommon who could share his regal delusions of privilege and persunal worth.

One rainy night, after a long journey to many

far-off bioregions, the prince nourished himself with a bowl of lentil-curry stew and confided his fears to his mother: "I don't think I'll ever find a genuine princess with whom to share my life, Mummy."

"Well, Son," the queen reassured him, "don't forget the many benefits of the single life. Don't let society and the church pressure you into a life-style for which you might not be suited."

"Perhaps I should widen my scope a bit," he mused.

"What? And throw out your standards?"

"No, Mummy, perhaps I have fallen into a trap of the orthodox heterosexualist majority. Maybe there is a fine young *prince* out there for me. It's at least worth a try."

Before his mother could answer, there was a knock on the castle door. The servants pulled open the heavy portal, and out of the rain stepped a young wommon, who was moisture-enhanced from head to foot. She was certainly attractive to the eye, if you're the type of shallow persun who attaches value to appearances. Luckily for our story, the prince was not one of those types. He had one standard, and only one standard, classist though it may have been.

Imagine the prince's surprise when the visitor blurted out, "A princess shouldn't be out in weather like this!" Well now, *this* was a revelation straight from the equine animal companion's mouth! The prince was struck orally inoperative for a moment, then invited the dryness-challenged visitor to enjoy their hospitality in the castle overnight.

While this was certainly a joyous development for the prince, his mother felt very threatened that someone was taking her son away from her. But rather than acknowledging the validity of her feelings and airing them in a constructive way, the queen decided on a ruse to test the visitor's claim.

She sneaked up to the bedchambers and found the room where the persun of saturation would be sleeping. She tore off all the bedding from the frame and placed one single pea on the bed slats. Then she placed 10 futons on top of the pea, and on top of that, 10 eiderdown quilts.

"There," said the queen. "If that drenched wench downstairs is really a princess, she will be refined enough to notice this lump and be unable to sleep."

The next morning at breakfast, over the royal granola, the queen innocently asked the young wommon how she had slept.

24

"Abominably," she replied. "I didn't get a wink all night."

The queen's eyes grew wide. Had her plan worked too well?

The visitor continued. "First of all, the bed was piled high with eiderdown quilts. Barbaric! How could I sleep, thinking of the poor geese who unwillingly surrendered their feathers for my comfort?"

The queen reddened a bit but said nothing.

"Then, as I was removing all the extra futons to share them with some of the less fortunate peasants living around the castle, I found a pea placed beneath them all. Shocking, with the state of the world as it is, that someone would waste food like that."

With these statements, the queen nearly choked on her soy milk. The prince, who had learned of his mother's scheme to screen out a princess, was so excited he couldn't keep silent any longer. "So you really are a princess!" he yelped.

"Last night I was, yes," she replied. The quizzical looks from the prince and queen led the wommon to elaborate: "Last night I was a princess; this morning I am an ancient Viking warrior. Oh, you sillies—I'm channeling! I have over a dozen past personalities that periodically inhabit my body—everyone from Charlemagne's mistress to Aesop's brother-in-law. And Cleopatra. But then, everyone's been Cleopatra at some time or other. Let me tell you, it makes for some interesting conversation at parties! It's all pretty exciting for an economically disadvantaged spoonmaker's daughter who grew up on the wrong side of the drainage ditch."

These revelations made the queen very angry, but the prince was intrigued. "So, when do you think you will be channeling a princess again?"

"A week from Tuesday," she said matter-of-factly, "mid-morning until early evening. I am very punctual with my past lives."

"Then on that Tuesday afternoon, I will ask you to be my wife and castle-mate, and you can rule by my side as an equal partner in every way."

The wommon considered a moment, then answered: "I would accept, if not for the fact that this morning, as I have said, I am a Viking warrior—Liefdahl by name, son of Ülfdahl—and I have a strong notion to lay siege to your castle just after breakfast." She calmly took a sip of coffee and grabbed another muffin.

"How rude!" said the queen with a slap on the

table. "We give her lodging in a storm and breakfast the next morning, and she swaps personalities on us and calmly talks about laying siege to us, without so much as a 'by your leave'!"

"Mother, please," said the prince. "Now, how long are you generally a Viking warrior?"

"Oh, not longer than 45 minutes."

"And after that?" he asked.

"After that, I'm usually St. Giles, living in a hovel and renouncing all worldly possessions."

"And that would include . . . ?"

"That would include"—the visitor smiled with a dawning awareness—"renouncing any and all worldly kingdoms conquered by my other spiritual co-habitators."

So, as is often the case, timing was crucial to a happy ending to our story. The "princess" and the prince were married the second Tuesday following, in accordance with her metaphysical timetable, and they had a very happy honeymoon, especially during certain transformations. Every time she became Liefdahl, son of Ülfdahl, she would conquer the prince and his castle, and every time she became St. Giles, she would give it right back. Channeling past lives and historical personalities became *de rigueur* in court from that day forward, and the queen, the prince, and the channeler lived a very happy life together, never quite knowing who would turn up at breakfast.

THE LITTLE
MER-PERSUN

way from the land, far from the shore and the effluent from stinking cities and corporate farms, was a habitat unlike any other in the world. Below the ocean surface, the plants grew in clusters of pink and red and yellow, and the long grasses swayed slowly in the current. Among these swam a host of colorful fishes, crustaceans, and arthropods in a stunning example of a healthy food chain. And amid all this teeming life flourished another race of creature, a unique and magnificent incarnation of biodiversity: the mer-people.

The mer-people had a king, and this king had seven daughters who all embodied to some degree the standards of attractiveness prevalent at that time. The one who best embodied these, however, was the youngest, who was named Calpurnia but nicknamed Kelpie. She was a very happy young sea-citizen, and she had the most pleasant singing voice that the mer-people had ever heard. She and her sisters were very close, and they all spent many hours collecting recyclables and jamming the sonar of whaling vessels.

The seven princesses loved to hear stories from their grand-mer-mother, especially about the mysterious folk who lived above the water's edge. Their grand-mer-mother told them about the old merchant ships that flew by, the forests and meadows filled with strange creatures, the bustling cities populated with persuns. The princesses could scarcely imagine such a place. They all laughed when their grand-mer-mother told them how the land people moved around on teetering pink stilts (those who were temporarily abled, of course) with fancy coverings on the ends to protect the stilts from wear. Their grand-mer-mother admonished them not to laugh at those unlucky enough to be born finless, but the princesses flicked their long tails and wondered how the land creatures could stand to look at themselves in the mirror.

The more stories they heard, the more curious the mer-sisters became. However, they were forbidden by mer-custom to swim to the surface on their own until their 15th birthdays. They weren't happy with this arrangement, but for the sake of cultural harmony, they agreed to abide by this restrictive rite of passage.

As the youngest in the family, Kelpie watched each of her mer-sisters swim to the surface on her 15th birthday and return with wondrous stories. One told of how humans were obsessed with making machines that saved themselves labor, then spent lots of money in special clubs for the privilege of keeping their muscles toned. One told of how they cut huge holes in their biggest trees, so they could examine Nature closely without leaving the comfort of their smoke-spewing metal sleds. One told of how the people built expensive electronic machines to help themselves sing in strange, shadowy places called karaoke bars.

But the little mer-persun was only mildly interested in learning how the other half breathed. She was content to explore her damp yet secure world,

31

play with the fish and other sea citizens, and grow in the confidence of her own mer-persunhood.

Soon the date of her 15th birthday arrived, and Kelpie was finally going to get her chance to view the surface world and engage in an open-minded cultural exchange. Since this rite of passage was as important from a sociological standpoint as her puberty in general, her mer-sisters and grand-mer-mother fussed over her greatly. Kelpie was generally not very vain, but she let her mer-kin adorn her with red seaweed, glittering coral, and bright oyster shells (always, of course, with the consent of the oysters). After all, there were so few rituals that feminine mer-persuns could call their own.

Bedecked in her finery, the little mer-persun swam away from her palace home toward the surface. The sun grew brighter and yellower as she rose, but the water also became murky and full of debris. When she finally broke through the surface, for the very first time in her life, she felt as though she needed a bath.

My, is it noisy above the water! she thought to herself. There were engines roaring, horns blowing, people shouting, and water splashing in a terrible cacophony. As she searched for the source of the din, she spun around and saw behind her a huge ship whose crew was firing powerful water hoses at a group of bearded men in a small rubber raft. The big ship was festooned with huge nets, cranes, and rigs, and the bearded men seemed to be steering their raft directly into its path. Kelpie was alarmed by the spectacle, but she had no idea what a life-and-non-life struggle it was until one man in the raft stood up and was knocked into the sea by a mighty blast from a water hose.

Always an altruistic sort, Kelpie dived without thinking and swam to rescue the man, who thrashed and screamed in the water. She came up from below and caught him just as he began to sink. When they made it back to the surface, he looked at his savior and could scarcely believe his eyes.

"Am I dead, or am I just crazy?" he asked.

"You're not dead, obviously," she said, "but as far as your mental health, I would leave such a diagnosis to a qualified professional."

"But you're . . . you're a mermaid!"

"Listen, buster," she said, the scales rising on her back, "another sexist remark like that and I'll let you swim home."

"No! I'm sorry, I wasn't thinking!"

"'Mer-persun' is the common term," Kelpie advised him, "although in my opinion it emphasizes the human part of our makeup at the expense of our fishness. It's an ongoing debate, you understand."

The little mer-persun examined this strange creature carefully. His hair was thicker in some places than in others, but unlike that of the otter or the sea elephant, it was scarcely enough to keep him warm or buoyant, and he was sorely blubber-deficient besides. His discomfort was obvious from the deep shade of purple his lips were turning.

"I must get you back to land before you freeze," Kelpie said. "Why were you pushed off your boat, anyway?"

"We were protesting drift-net fishing, and that Russian trawler decided that they could do whatever they wanted to us, since we were in international waters. But we got the bastards on videotape, so they're in trouble now."

She thought to herself, *What a strange phrase, "international waters,"* then said to him, "Your efforts to defend the ocean's ecosystem are commendable, but you almost became shark food yourself."

He looked dreamily into her eyes. "None of that

matters now. You are the most beautiful creature I have ever seen."

"Oh, don't talk bilge."

"What's your name? Mine's Dylan."

"My name is Calpurnia, but my friends call me Kelpie."

"I am so taken by your beauty and kindness, Kelpie. I love you. I want to stay with you forever."

"It wouldn't work. See, your fingers are already turning pruney."

"But if I can't stay here, why don't you come live with me? I can make my house mer-accessible with flumes and chutes. I could even introduce you to Phillipe Cousteau—he can make you a star."

"Hold on, finless," she said, turning angry. "You air breathers are really full of yourselves, aren't you? You don't love me. You just want to show me off to all your friends. 'See what an eco-friendly stud I am? I'm living with a mer-persun!' Why in all the sea would I want to join your private aquarium? I can hear the jokes now: 'Where can I get me some of that bait?'; 'I love a little tail'; 'Hey, baby, wanna spawn?' Forget it, Greenpeace boy, I'm not some trophy you can claim from the sea and mount."

The surface dweller didn't have much of anything

to say after this. His teeth were chattering and his eyes were glazing over as he reached the more advanced stages of hypothermia. Even with his terra-centric attitude, the mer-persun felt pity for Dylan in his primate-out-of-land position, and she headed for shore as fast as she could. Meanwhile, the men on the rubber raft successfully stopped the Russian trawler by jamming the raft into its propellers and causing a boiler to explode aboard ship, which sent all the crew members and the ecowarriors to a watery yet commendable grave.

The little mer-persun, dodging sinister drift nets and massive, churning cruise ships, tried to find a secluded shoreline where she could throw the human back. However, rampant beachfront and wetlands development made this nearly impossible until she found one rocky cove with a small sandy beach. Before the man could wake up, Kelpie swam off, not wishing to endure any more emotional scenes, cultural imperialism, or Jungian archetypes.

Back home she told her whole mer-family about her adventures on the surface. Of course, she left out Dylan's profession of love and his ideas for a life together, which (the more she thought about it) involved nothing but great sacrifice on her part and numerous benefits for him. Besides, Kelpie found the whole idea rather repulsive. Her mer-family applauded her selfless, she-roic efforts.

Some months passed and the little mer-persun gave barely a thought to the air breather she'd saved. She was too busy with her music lessons and her algae garden to consider a relationship with someone who wore clothes and walked on two feet.

One day a courier from the castle swam up to Kelpie in her garden and breathlessly announced that her presence was desired in court immediately. Wondering whatever could be the matter, she hurried to the royal hall. There she found her mer-father, her grand-mer-mother, her mer-sisters, and many royal advisers and drifters-on. And in front of the mer-king swam a strange pink creature—bulky and armored and shaped like a macaroon.

"Daughter, come forward," intoned the mer-king in a properly regal tone. "This visitor requests an audience with you." When the stranger drifted around, Kelpie's jaw nearly hit bottom. It was Dylan, the eco-defender she had saved from drowning!

"Greetings, Kelpie," he said.

"Dylan! But what . . . what's happened to the rest of you?" she asked.

"I've had myself turned into a denizen of the sea. It's amazing what they can do with gene splicing these days."

"But in the name of Poseidon, *why?*"

"To prove my sincere devotion and love for you, of course."

"No, I mean, why did you choose to become half-man, half-*prawn*?"

Dylan sighed. "It's a long story, involving government restrictions on research and chromosome compatibility and so forth. But I gotta tell you, I love my new hard shell and eyestalks. Look, I can read both pages of a book at the same time!" He demonstrated his new ocular talents for everyone assembled.

"But you've sacrificed your peopleness," Kelpie said. "What about your family and friends?"

"Who needs 'em? Buncha primates. I've always felt more at home on the ocean, only now I'm *in* the ocean. And today, seeing you here in the salt water, I love you even more."

"I'm very touched. I . . . I don't know what to say," she stammered, utterly captivated by his deep and selfless sacrifice.

Dylan turned to face the throne and summoned

up all the dignity he could in his bulky pink frame. "Your Majesty, I'd like to ask for your daughter's hand in marriage."

The mer-king replied royally, "What kind of sexist operation do you think we're running here? Ask her yourself, shrimp."

He turned to the little mer-persun and asked, "Calpurnia, will you marry me?"

What could Kelpie say but yes? She could've said no, she wanted to continue her education and establish a career. She could've said no, she didn't approve of scientific augmentation or changes between species. She could've said no, she was allergic to shellfish. She could've said no a thousand different ways, but happily she said yes.

Kelpie and Dylan were married soon after that and begat a fine school of fry. In a few years time, Kelpie became more involved in affairs of state and sang occasionally for the entertainment of their friends, while Dylan continued his eco-defense activities, this time from below the water. And while their life together wasn't a bed of coral every day, they always taught their spawn to be happy and proud of their multi-cultural, multi-genus heritage.

THE TORTOISE AND THE HARE

f all the boastful and self-important animals, the worst in all the countryside (apart from the humans, of course) was the hare. He would talk on and on about his swiftness, sleekness, and superior muscle tone with anyone unfortunate enough to be nearby. What's more, he continually derided the other animals that didn't share his obsession with fleeting physical "perfection."

One of his frequent targets for ridicule was the tortoise, who with his stout yet functional legs, lower metabolism, and overall endomorphic body shape stood (or rather squatted) in marked contrast to the hare. The tortoise, perfectly content to take on life at his own speed, always insisted his metabolism was as efficient as anyone else's.

The hare, however, continually taunted the tortoise while he struck poses and flexed his pecs. "Hey, low-rider," he said, "I bet you can make extra money (*huff-huff*) renting yourself out as a paperweight (*huff-huff, preen-preen*)!"

The tortoise smiled patiently. "Thank you for the advice, my velocity-fortified friend."

"Come on, stumpy," goaded the hare, "can't you rise up when someone (*huff-huff*) throws down the gauntlet?"

"I can't see how gauntlet abuse has anything to do with me," said the tortoise, who had apparently achieved slowness in more than one aspect of his character. "I enjoy my inertia and would rather just sit and watch the world go by."

"Ooooh, how can you be so content?" fumed the hare. "You're just so smug (*huff-huff*), I challenge you to a race to show you the consequences and (*preen-preen*) health risks of such a sedentary lifestyle."

The tortoise was appalled. "A . . . *competition?*"

He almost choked on the word. "Just to prove that one of us is somehow *better* than the other? What kind of example is that to set? I'll have no part of it."

Some other animals that were standing nearby overheard this conversation and began to listen with interest.

"What's the matter (*preen-preen*), are you . . . ?" The hare caught himself and looked around, then said in a softer voice, "Are you chicken?"

At this, the tortoise grew angry. "Now listen, if you're going to start insulting other species to cover up your own insecurities . . ."

"Come on, doorstop," taunted the hare. "Are you really compassionate for pullets or just plain scared?"

A crowd of animals had now gathered and was, to use another poultry-exploitative phrase, egging on both combatants. Some were eager for the hare to be put in his place, others wanted to see the tortoise's self-righteous bubble popped, and still others were the unreflective couch-potato types who craved constant stimulation.

With pressure coming from all sides, the tortoise felt a tug-of-war between his principles against competition and the need to teach the hare a lesson. Finally, and without a trace of irony, he said, "All right, I'll race you. And what's more, I'll win, just to prove to you that winning isn't everything."

Preparations for the big event began immediately. The tortoise and the hare agreed to appoint the fox as Commissioner of Kinetic Wellness and Overland Velocity Contests. It was the fox's duty to establish the route and duration of the race, as well as work out the details for the merchandising and pay-per-view revenue. There was some talk about adding biking and swimming meets to the footrace, but it was decided that interest in such an "Iron Animal" competition wouldn't be as high.

The hare and the tortoise began to train in earnest for Race Day. Some ignorant commentators assumed that all members of the rabbit family were fast, due to their genetic inheritance, limber body, and well-developed thigh muscles. The hare rightly took exception to these prejudices because they ignored his many hours of hard work and sacrifice. To counter them, his training camp was always open to the media and his supporters, who cheered him on as he cross-trained. This also kept the persistent rumors of blood-doping and amphetamine abuse to a manageable and deniable size. For his part, the tortoise prepared by carbo-loading and watching training films.

As the hype for the big showdown escalated, the imagination of the other animals in the countryside was absolutely (and somewhat unhealthily) focused on the race. Depending on their individual temperaments, the animals were rabidly and obsessively either pro-tortoise or pro-hare. Many a friendship, marriage, and other significant interanimal relationship was tested in the days leading up to the race.

The hare zealots—generally more youthful animals who were impressed solely by style, speed, and hipness—strutted around in specially licensed T-shirts with the slogans "Just Jump It" and "Rabbitude!"

Fans of the tortoise praised his defense of principle against tremendous odds, as well as his self-deprecating wit and acceptance of his alternative body image. They expressed their support by donning baseball caps stitched with the words "Eat my dust, bunny!"

A small but vocal non-majority opposed the entire notion of holding a race at all. They wrote op-ed pieces, phoned in to radio talk shows, and even distributed a poster that read, "RACES are not HEALTHY for kids, colts, kittens, pups, chicks, ducklings, cygnets, eaglets, hatchlings, calves, cubs, fawns, lambkins, piglets, joeys, tadpoles, and other living things." Their efforts were to no avail, however, and the day of the big race soon arrived.

The air crackled with anticipation that morning as the crowds gathered at the starting gate. Vendors were there, selling chipatis, juices, and energy-supplement bars. Promoters were there, giving away phone cards, sports drinks, and cereal samples emblazoned with pictures of the tortoise and the hare. Newscasters and TV technicians were there, in droves of elaborate electronic vans, to exploit every last detail and image of "this story about the simplest of all challenges—to race."

Hardly anyone noticed when the tortoise arrived. He was so unassuming and free of ostentation that he blended in easily with the crowd. The serene look on his face was puzzling, considering the long odds he was up against.

As you might expect, the arrival of the hare and his entourage could not be described as humble or restrained. It was hard to miss the long black limousine that edged its way through the crowd, or the cheers that erupted when the doors flew open and out stepped the hare, with a starlet on each arm and surrounded by four beefy bodyguards (or animal protection professionals, as they preferred to be called). The rowdier elements of the crowd tried to get close to the hare, but his muscular interdiction force kept them at bay.

The hare stepped up to the starting line, raised his hands to the crowd, and took off his gold lamé warm-up suit. He gulped a big swallow of the sports drink he was endorsing and ate a fistful of his authorized breakfast cereal with a smile. He then turned to the tortoise with a menacing look in his eye.

"I'm gonna pound you so bad, tortoise, (*huff*) it'll make lying on your back feel like a vacation."

Whether or not he meant to offend any of the optically challenged members of the crowd, the tortoise just smiled and said, "We'll see."

The starter for the race, having been enjoined not to use a pistol, a cannon, the word "BANG!" or any other violent inducement to run, held a red handkerchief at arm's length, let it hang there a few seconds, then dropped it with a flourish. Instantly, the hare was off in a lightning blaze of speed. The tortoise moseyed off at a more natural pace, ever mindful that most sports injuries arise from inadequate preparation and abrupt starts and stops.

With cheering throngs on either side, the hare sped down the course like quicksilver. By the time he was out of town and in the countryside, he had long lost sight of his competitor. So confident was he in his velocity prerogative over the tortoise that he decided to accept the invitation of one of the film crews and grant an interview about his mid-race thoughts, reminiscences of childhood, and hopes for the future.

Meanwhile, the tortoise plodded on, carefully replenishing his bodily fluids with the cups of isotonic liquid that were provided along the route. He soon found himself hitting what runners call "the wall," but the encouragement from the crowd and his own strength of will helped him push through it until he entered the "zone." It was a good thing, too, since at that point he was only 30 meters from the starting line.

The hare chatted amiably about himself with the interviewer and, since he was talking about his favorite subject, the time flew by. When it was all wrapped up and the hare stepped out from the trailer, he heard cheering coming from the direction of the finish line. He bounded down the course, touched by the idea that the crowd was warming up to welcome him. But when he finally caught sight of the end, what did he see but the tortoise crossing the finish line!

The hare ran as fast as he could, but he couldn't pass the tortoise in time and had to settle for "finishing almost fastest." He began to scream and pound his fists, complain about the officiating, demand a recall of the commissioner, challenge the tortoise to a urine test, and threaten to sue for millions in lost endorsement revenue. The tortoise just wanly smiled as he tried to power down.

Meanwhile, to celebrate the victory, fans of both the tortoise and the hare, as well as various bystanders and hangers-on, smashed shop windows, looted electronics and jewelry stores, overturned cars, and set fire to anything that was handy. By the time the police broke up the crowds with recycled rubber bullets and biodegradable pepper gas, they had arrested 57 animals for over-enthusiastic celebrating.

While such destructive merrymaking was deplorable (and certainly depended on many socioeconomic influences), the most shocking part of the story was yet to come. Both racers did submit to urinalysis, and the results were not good for the tortoise, who was found to be a heavy user and abuser of steroids. The tortoise claimed that it was really the aftereffect of an asthma medication, but the fox, in his role as Commissioner of Kinetic Wellness and Overland Velocity Contests, was forced to disqualify him and proclaim the hare as "finishing most fastest."

In response to this scandalous news, fans of both the tortoise and the hare, as well as various bystanders and hangers-on, smashed shop windows, looted electronics and jewelry stores, overturned cars, and set fire to anything that was handy. This time the police arrested 115 animals for over-enthusiastic celebrating.

It was soon decided that footraces, pawraces, hoofraces, and other such competitions only inflamed the animal populace and unleashed emotions that were not nurturant of public harmony. The fox resigned his position and was immediately named the new Facilitator of Constructive, Cooperative Kinetic Pastimes. His department heavily promoted participation in noncompetitive activities such as snorkeling, water ballet, hackey sack, and duck-duck-goose (for any and all species). Further, he decreed any animal found to be competing with his or her neighbor in any type of sport or contest was to be disciplined with several hours of community service and forced to listen to audiotapes of the various sportscasters giving their analysis of the big race between the tortoise and the hare.

PUSS IN BOOTS

n a land not so very far away lived a man and his three sons. After the father had achieved his inevitable non-essentialness, his estate was divided among his sons: The eldest inherited the oil company, the next eldest got the publishing and media holdings, and the least eldest got a cat. Forgetting for a moment the hours of companionship and contentment that an animal companion can bring, the least eldest son pleaded with his brothers not to compel him to contest the will in probate.

"Listen, brothers," he said, "while you'll be able to support yourselves with your share of the inheritance, I'll be lucky if I can breed this cat or put it in commercials. Don't force me to sell him to a cosmetics company just to get a return on my assets."

His brothers ignored him and told him to have his lawyer call their lawyers, but the cat obviously took offense at these flip remarks. Later the cat scolded this cruel, shortsighted human: "It's just like your kind to treat someone with four legs like a resource for you to exploit. We're not put here for your enrichment, bub, material or otherwise. In fact, I'm so disgusted that now I'm not going to tell you how I was going to make you a great and powerful persun."

More than the fact that the cat could speak, these last words sparked the interest of the ambitious yet meagerly synapsed young man: "Oh, Mr. Puss, my dearest and most trusted friend, how did you plan to do this?"

"I don't think you want to know. You obviously haven't the foresight and fortitude it would take for a successful career in public service."

"Oh, please," said the winningly eager young man. "I'd love to go into politics. I'm not much suited for anything else, and my brothers might be able to give us a jump-start in the contributions area."

The cat sighed. "My heart does go out to you," said Puss, "a poor idiot left on his own. Very well, I will help you. For me to get started, I need two things: first, a blue pinstripe suit—Armani, nothing less—plus a briefcase and some fancy stitched cowboy boots; and second, a promise that you'll never make a single solitary utterance in public without my OK."

The wholesome-looking young man readily agreed, since he never had much that was important or original to say anyway. He took the cat to a fancy haberdasher to be outfitted properly. When this was done, the cat told him, "Go home now and wait. Practice looking statesman-like by riding horses, playing touch football, writing your memoirs, things like that."

"But I don't have any memoirs to write," protested the ruggedly handsome young man.

"I said *practice* writing," the cat reiterated, pointing a claw. "If you think you'll ever have the chance to do your own writing, then we've got a problem already." With that, Puss in Boots left to call his first press conference.

The primaries for the senate race were only five weeks away at this point, and the field of candidates was already quite crowded. When Puss in Boots held his press conference, only a handful of reporters had the time or interest to show up. This hardly mattered, since it was to be rather short anyway.

All the cat did was walk to the podium and say, "I'd like to announce that my employer is not a candidate for the party nomination for the senate seat at this time. Thank you. No questions, please." Then he walked away.

And was the reaction tremendous! Breathless articles and news reports began to appear about the reluctant candidate. Who was he? What did he stand for? What was the significance of the public groundswell that surrounded this strapping figure of youthful vitality? With just the slightest spin doctoring and some wise use of media time, Puss in Boots proceeded to forge the image of his human companion as a man forced into public life by the will of the people, who were disillusioned and were looking for a white knight (colorist though such concepts are) on a tall fiery charger (ditto heightist and speciesist, not to mention quite Eurocentric overall).

Within a few weeks and without uttering a word, the young man with the Redfordesque good looks won the party nomination for the senate!

"Wow! I can't believe it," said the malleable candidate. "I guess I'd better start figuring out my position on the issues."

"You do and I'll break your neck," hissed the cat. "Let me worry about your positions, as well as your beliefs and your off-the-cuff remarks and your spontaneity and everything else. You just remember: Don't say a thing unless I tell you to."

Now Puss in Boots began to work in earnest to get his meal ticket elected to the senate. He issued position papers that were totally pointless yet exquisitely quotable. He had the candidate photographed shaking hands with factory workers, retirees, and customers at luncheonettes. They challenged the incumbent to a debate and then backed out at the last minute, declaring that such an event would be just an exercise in "politics as usual." Their optimistically simple campaign slogan—"It's Time for a Change!"—seemed to strike a chord with the optimistically simple voters.

Throughout the frenzy of the campaign, no one noticed or commented on Puss in Boots's lack of credentials. In fact, seduced by his easy and apparently candid manner, no one ever noticed that he was of feline descent at all. It just demonstrated the commentator's observation, "In the land of the optically challenged, the monocularly gifted individual is first in line at the trough."

Election day drew near, with all the mudslinging and innuendo you could imagine. Puss in Boots's candidate, however, with his easy confidence and glint in the eye, seemed somehow to rise above the fray. This might have been due to the fact that he was still forbidden to speak his mind (or what there was of it) in any way, shape, or form. Puss in Boots, on the other hand, was always available to the media and ready with a charming, folksy anecdote or some evidence that their opponent had undergone electroshock therapy to stop the temporary lapses into dementia that made him want to release all the criminals from prison with a $50 gift certificate and an automatic pistol.

As the campaign came down to the wire, and with his heartland–born-and-bred candidate lagging in the polls, Puss knew it was time to stop playing footsie. He called another press conference and this time announced to the media, "Our campaign honorably requests that our opponent step down from the race, so that we won't have to disclose possible evidence we may have found that might link our opponent to an experimental, gender-reversing medical procedure he may have undergone 23 years ago in an undisclosed overseas country, where the majority of the population speaks Swedish. Thank you. No questions, please."

This insinuation, as you may have guessed, turned the entire campaign around. Rumors flew about the type of evidence Puss and his boss may or may not have had. Their opponent repeatedly denied accusations that he had once been a wommon and was now a man, that he was still a wommon now trapped in a man's body, or that he was now a man trapped in a wommon's body with a penchant for cross-dressing—not that there is anything wrong or unnatural, certainly, with any of these lifestyle choices.

As usual, emotions rather than reason carried the day, and after all the ballots were counted on election day, Puss in Boots and his ruddy, exuberant human companion had won by a comfortable margin.

At the victory party, Puss pulled the new senator aside and said to him, "You see? I told you I could be useful to you. You may not have the wealth of your brothers yet, but you soon will have, and even more clout, if you play your cards right. There is even some talk—initiated by me, of course—that you're going to run for president in the next election because the country's problems are too urgent and your ideas are too big to be penned up in the senate. What do you think of that?"

"Oh, my skillful, cunning cat," he said, "I can't thank you enough. Please accept my apologies for ever contemplating selling you to perfume researchers."

"Just do as I say," said Puss in Boots, taking a sip of his designer water, "and instead of the stealth candidate, they'll be calling you . . . Mr. President. Now, you better get up there and give them the victory speech I wrote for you."

The beaming politician entered the crowd to cheers and applause and pushed his way forward to the podium. "To my family, friends, and supporters," he began, "I want to thank you all for your hard work and dedication, and I'm pleased to tell you I have just received a phone call from my opponent conceding the election!"

Applause, applause, applause!

"He was a worthy adversary and fought the good fight, but this campaign was not about issues or ideology, or even ability or brainpower. It was about the plain and simple message: It's time for a change!"

Applause, applause, applause!

"And now, if you'll let me, I'd like to depart from my prepared comments." From the wings came the sounds of a glass shattering and a low, painful groan. He continued, "I'd like to thank someone without whom this victory wouldn't have been possible: my campaign adviser, my confidante, and I'm proud to say, my cat—Puss in Boots!"

Applause, applau . . . *silence.*

Had they heard him right? This Kennedyesque young man, their bright and shining knight, their hope for the future, had let his *cat* run the campaign? Not that it was unprecedented—other non-human animals had held high appointed positions for years—but why had he kept it a secret? What kind of a man was he to hide such information, and what else was he hiding?

"Puss," he said, "come out here and take a bow."

Puss in Boots just stood in the wings, shaking his head, his paw over his eyes. He had had his doubts, but he never wanted to believe his master was so cerebrally undercapitalized as to spill the legumes at his own victory party.

The people in the crowd grew angry, even the cat lovers. They felt they'd been deceived, cheated, jilted, cuckolded. They started to boo, tear down banners, and pop balloons as they began to look for payback. The new senator had to make his escape through the rear behind the rostrum. He looked for his cat everywhere with no luck. Then, over in a corner, he saw a group of reporters and cameras gathered around, and there was Puss in Boots right in the center of them.

By the time the senator got to where the press had clustered around Puss, all he could hear was his cat saying, " . . . to apologize to everyone who worked on this campaign and put their trust in this candidate, and also to you, you hardworking reporters. Had I known this pathetic schemer to be so . . . unstable and . . . duplicitous, I would never have become involved with his campaign. I hereby resign from his staff before any other damage is inflicted on the electoral system, or on the hearts and minds of the public. Thank you. No questions, please."

The reporters ran off to file their stories. Puss in Boots walked slowly up to his former employer and said, "If only you'd stuck to the script. Good luck in office, if you survive the recount."

"But I don't understand," said the beleaguered senator. "No one figured out you were a *cat* before now?"

Puss looked him straight in the eye. "Do the words 'credibility problem' mean anything to you? Nobody really *cares* that I'm a cat—not on the record, anyway—but now because of your slip of the brain, it looks like a big cover-up. Fraud, nepotism, interspecies exploitation—your squeaky-clean image is kaput. If you *had* to tell them, a weepy confession would've been much better than a bungled disclosure. That's Spin Doctoring 101, but you're working with such low wattage, it slipped right by you."

Puss in Boots bid the man farewell and walked away. He wrote a few magazine articles to tell his side of the sordid story, then got a job as a television pundit based in the capital. The senator barely survived the inevitable recall vote, but questions about his judgment lingered and impeded any effectiveness in office he might have had over the next six years. Almost from the day he was sworn in, he was treated like a non-ambulatory waterfowl, something Puss in Boots reminded him and the rest of the country about every time the pundit cat went on the air.

SLEEPING PERSUN OF BETTER-THAN-AVERAGE ATTRACTIVENESS

ong, long ago, there lived a king and a queen, two equal partners in life who shared everything—including the fervent wish to have a baby. (This was much easier for the king, of course, since he would never have to endure the upheavals of pregnancy, the pain of childbirth, and the miseries of postpartum depression. You could rightly call his wish more vicarious than hers.) But as many times as the king would inflict his baser instincts on the queen, they (or, more accurately, *she*) remained childless.

One day, as the queen bathed in a nearby river, a frog leaped onto the lily pad next to her. Then, to her amazement, the frog cleared its throat and spoke.

"Although it's probably not a good idea to bring another human being into the world," said the amphibious messenger, "I know of your conception problems and would like to help. If you follow my advice, you will soon be with child."

"Oh, such joyous news!" trilled the queen. "What must I do to prepare myself, frog?! What must I do?! Tell me!!"

"Your best bet is to go the natural route, and for pity's sake, learn to relax! Get some regular exercise, eat more greens and grains, and eliminate animal fat from your diet. Later, if you need one, I can recommend a good lactation consultant."

So the queen did as the frog directed, and on the next full cycle of the moon, her body was colonized by the seed of the exploitative monarchy.

Nine months later (not to minimize the physical strain on the queen in the interim), a healthy pink pre-wommon was welcomed into the castle. Many gender-neutral names were considered for her, such as Connor, Tucker, and Taylor, that might have lessened any sexual discrimination she would encounter on her career path (for, while she was born a princess, her parents would never presume to limit her future to one of mindless leisure and privilege). After talking to a few image consultants, they decided to give her the name Rosamond.

The king was so happy and so proud of his now-obvious potency that he ordered a huge banquet to be held. Special guests from all over the kingdom came and feasted on exotic fruits, rare vegetables, and whole-grain casseroles (although nobody touched the lovely placenta paella). The most special of all the guests were 12 magickally accomplished womyn, famous throughout the land for their wisdom and their rejection of the hegemony of analytic Western rationalism. After the feast, each wommon walked up to the persun of newbornness and gave her a blessing.

"May this pre-wommon be blessed with a body image with which she is comfortable," said the first.

"May she have a keen analytical mind that also leaves room for intuition and inspiration," said the next.

"May she have good math skills," said the third, and so on down the line.

But either through oversight or superstition, the king failed to invite the 13th member of this magick sorority. Humiliated by this snub, she snuck into the gathering and hid in the shadows, nurturing her resentment. When she could stand it no longer, she pushed her way to the center of the crowd and was up-front with her emotions: "So you think you can create the perfect persun with all your blessings? Not if I can help it!" She strode up to the royal bassinet and said to tiny Rosamond, "May you grow up thinking you can't be complete without a man, put unrealistic hopes of perfect and total happiness on your marriage, and become a bored, dissatisfied, and unfulfilled housewife!"

Everyone in the room gasped in fright! How could anyone be so morally out of the mainstream to wish such a terrible fate on a defenseless child? The 13th wommon cackled in a manner that just happened to be maniacal and, ignoring everyone's pleas to stay and talk through their differences, disappeared into the shadows.

Luckily for little Rosamond, the 13th magickal wommon had long ago rejected the validity of empirical scientific thought, and as a result had forgotten how to count. The vengeful sorceron did not realize that the *12th* magickal wommon had not yet given her blessing on the child. While this wise and kind sister could not undo what had been done, she could lessen the agony of this terrible curse. She walked up to the pre-adult and said, "When you are just reaching the prime of puberty, may you prick your finger on a spinning wheel and fall asleep for 100 years. By that time, perhaps men will be more evolved and your pain in finding a progressive, affirming lifemate will not be so great."

With all these supernatural blessings, curses, and overrides, the king became so fearful for his daughter that he ordered every spinning wheel in the kingdom destroyed. Deprived of a means of producing any fabric, the people of the kingdom were forced to devise new ways of reusing old clothing, and thus reduced their conspicuous consumption and eased the burden on their landfills.

As the years passed, Rosamond grew into an intelligent, compassionate, and self-actualized young wommon. Whether she was also physically attractive is of no importance here and also depends entirely on one's standard of beauty. It also perpetuates the myth that all princesses are beautiful, and that their beauty gives them liberty over the fates of others. So, please, don't even bring up the fact that she was quite a looker.

One day, when her parents were off on a retreat to learn to release their "inner peasant," Rosamond began to explore her castle. She came upon a doorway she had never seen before, which led to a winding stairway up into a tower. At the top of the tower was a little room, where Rosamond found a temporally advanced wommon busy at her spinning wheel.

"What are you doing, sister?" Rosamond asked.

"Recapturing the means of production and staking ground in my own economic empowerment," she replied sweetly.

"It looks like fun, yet also educational and enriching; may I try?" But no sooner had Rosamond touched the wheel than her finger was severely pricked. And before she could decide whether alyssum or lobelia tincture would make the best balm for the wound, she fell into a deep state of non-wakability.

And at the instant Rosamond fell asleep, in an inspiring display of solidarity, everyone in the castle also began to slumber. The environmental hygienist stopped scrubbing the floor, the domestic engineer stopped dusting, the laundron stopped washing the clothes, and all fell asleep right where they were. Even the nonhuman animal residents—while they certainly weren't bound to obey or emulate the humans—stopped in their tracks and nodded off.

Around the castle the grounds were left untouched and reverted to their natural wildness. As the castle's inhabitants slept, thorn bushes grew thickly and heavily year after year, so that soon they blocked passage to the castle and eventually obscured it from view entirely. This vibrant new bio-district would have gone unmolested, if not for the lustful and destructive natures of the males in the surrounding kingdoms. Legends grew about the castle and the sleeping princess therein—who now had become an unsurpassed beauty in the wish-fulfilling stories that the men recounted. Many young princes, in a rush of hubris and testosterone, sought to disrupt the thorny ecosystem and awaken the princess, as if she were just some windup doll waiting for the man with the right key. But no sooner did these foolhardy adventurers push their way through the vegetation than the thorn bushes closed tight, ensnaring the men until they returned to the earth from which they came.

Then, after 100 years, through the region rode another prince (and please don't ask how charming he was, either). He had heard about the environmentally friendly castle and its REM-enhanced inhabitants, and was intrigued by the idea of a place so at peace with itself. He dismounted from his trusty equine companion and walked up to the thick hedge. With a creak and a rustle, it opened to let him pass, and he walked through its verdant portal. Once inside the castle, the prince marvelled at the stillness around him. All the people, all the animals, all the birds—even the fire in the grate—were perfectly motionless. Amazed by all this self-control, the prince believed he had stumbled upon a top-notch meditation center and rejoiced, for he was a pilgrim dedicated to self-improvement and transcendence to the Absolute Reality. He began to search the grounds for the sensory deprivation tanks, then found the door to the tower and ascended the stairs.

When he opened the door to Rosamond's room and saw her lying there, the prince marvelled at her serenity and composure. He knew immediately that she was the one responsible for the enlightenment of the castle. Eager to learn from such a venerable mistress, he touched her on the arm, then tapped her, then poked her, then shook her, then jostled her. "She is in such a deep meditative state that the outside world completely falls away for her," said the prince. "Oh, I must follow this teacher!" To show his reverence, he crawled to the foot of her cot, kissed her slippered foot, and settled into a lotus position.

Immediately Rosamond began to stir. She coughed and smacked her lips numerous times, trying to get rid of the taste of 100 years of morning mouth. She sat up and saw the figure sitting at the end of her cot, and instantly something changed inside her. All of Rosamond's independence, education, and previous persunal growth fell away like a cloak, and she swooned like a starlet in a cheap melodrama. "My prince, you have awakened me!" she chirped loudly.

The prince was awestruck. He didn't realize what he had done, and hardly had the breath to say, "Oh, I beg your forgiveness, teacher. I did not want to disturb your meditation. I seek only your guidance . . ."

"But I am not your teacher," she giggled. "I am your princess, and you have come to take me away from all this, make me your bride, bring me to a big castle with a white picket fence, and let me live happily ever after!"

"Take you away? From this Shangri-la, this Utopia? But your entire castle is a huge vortex of positive energy, the perfect place to expand our consciousness and pursue individual nothingness."

"What are you talking about? Come and kiss me!"

"Kiss you?" he asked in a very disappointed voice. "Oh, teacher, how carnal! You do not think me worthy of enlightenment."

"But you are the only man who could arrive here and break the spell," she cried. "We were fated to be together."

"Teacher, you should know there is no such thing as fate," corrected the prince, "only our unique destinies, and if we are lucky, a little synchronicity thrown in here and there."

"Don't use such big words," Rosamond pouted. "Didn't you come here to marry me and make me a fulfilled wommon?"

The prince thought for a second, then looked panicked. "Teacher, please! Your riddles are too much for a neophyte such as I. Be patient with me, I beg you."

"A hundred years is long enough to be patient," she insisted. "It's bad enough that none of my friends will be alive to come to my wedding, but on top of that, I get a prince who doesn't want to get physical, only metaphysical."

The prince looked supremely lost. This was certainly not how he'd envisioned a meeting with an exalted teacher. "I don't know about you," he said with a sigh, "but I could really go for a nice, soothing colonic."

The frustrated Rosamond begged the prince to be her mate, but her tears, bribes, and threats could not move him. The prince, who wanted to get in touch with his own emotions rather than hers, continued to beseech her for her knowledge and insights (which were rather scanty, as you might understand, despite her 116 years on the planet). With their arguing, they stayed up long into the night, as did the rest of the castle after such a monumental cat-nap. And so, with this sad standoff, the prophecies of the 12th sister of sorcery, as well as those of the 13th, were fulfilled.

THE CITY MOUSE AND THE SUBURBAN MOUSE

 mouse who lived in the suburbs had an old friend who lived in the city. One day he invited his friend to come out for a visit. The city mouse readily accepted the invitation, eager to see his pal and enjoy some greenery for a change. So on the duly appointed day, he walked to the central mass-transit dispatch point and took a train out to the end of the line.

Upon arrival in the suburbs, the city mouse began to look for his friend's house. Of course, he was used to straight, numbered streets and quickly got lost amidst the wide lawns, curving roads, and cul-de-sacs. After several hours of searching through the Valley Dales and Dally Vales, the Nettle Brooks and Breton Nooks, by sheer luck he found his friend's address.

The suburban mouse had gone to great lengths to make this a memorable visit, even buying a big floral centerpiece to match the napkins and placemats on his table. He'd laid out a sizable feast for his guest—macaroni and cheese, creamed corn, even Jell-O salad with mandarin orange wedges. The city mouse ate a bit of each dish but couldn't help showing his disdain for such mundane fare. The unnatural quiet was also beginning to get to him; the only sounds he could hear were the clicks of lawn sprinklers and the roar of distant riding mowers. After dinner, the suburban mouse handed the city mouse a no-alcohol light beer and suggested that they do a little channel surfing to pass the time.

The city mouse said, "My friend, life is too short to live this way. Look at you! Your food is dull, your entertainment is dull, even your hairstyle is 15 years behind the times."

The suburban mouse was taken aback, especially by the comment about his hairstyle. "Heavens, what should I do?"

"Come visit me in the city next week," was the reply, "and we'll enjoy more diversity and excitement than you've ever dreamed of. I'll show you the life that's fit for a healthy young mouse!"

So the next week, the suburban mouse headed into the city. He was a little late arriving because it took him $2\frac{1}{2}$ hours to find a parking space. As he stepped out of his car, he was asked for a monetary donation by someone supporting himself outside the reigning capitalist paradigm. The vehement language and uncompromising natural aroma of this street citizen startled the suburban mouse, who fell over backward into the gutter. After he picked himself up from the grime, two police officers began to harass him about interfering with the "quality of life" in the neighborhood and inquired whether he would be so kind as to refrain from showing his stupid face around there again or he'd be buying himself a mess of trouble. The suburban mouse sagely took their advice and trotted away. A half-block away from his friend's apartment, the visitor was interrupted by a former client of the correctional system, who liberated the mouse's watch and wallet in return for the gracious offer of letting him walk away in one piece.

Shaken, sore, and spun around, the suburban mouse finally reached his friend's building. No sooner had he done so than the city mouse ran down the front steps.

"Where ya been? C'mon, we'll be late for our dinner reservations."

"But I," he squeaked breathlessly, his paw over his heart, "I was just mugged and—"

"Ah, fuhgetabouddit!"

And the two of them rushed off to dinner. The city mouse had chosen a new, exclusive restaurant that combined the cuisines of Jamaica and Tibet in an original way (its most popular dish was the jerk yak). There was a long line of customers waiting outside the restaurant, but the mice enjoyed a private dining area in the alley by the kitchen. They feasted on scraps of some of the finest and costliest fare in the entire city. The suburban mouse didn't recognize any of the food, and wouldn't have been able to pronounce the names if he had, but he was thoroughly enjoying himself. His earlier troubles faded into the background as he gobbled away hungrily next to his friend. Then they slipped out for cappuccino and cannolis.

The suburban mouse was entranced by all the activity and diversity around him—all the yelling and laughing, cars honking, music playing. Nighttime in the city seemed even more vibrant and alive than daytime in the suburbs. A vast, wonderful panorama he never knew existed was unfolding before him with dazzling speed.

On the way home, in front of the tropical pet and retread tire store, a pair of unlicensed sex workers tried to engage them in conversation. "Hey, fellas, how about a little transaction in the personal services sector?" said one with refreshing candor about the true nature of all male-female relationships.

The suburban mouse thought this was all marvelously colorful and authentic, and he began to ask the sex-care providers where on earth they went shopping for their boots. The city mouse, not wishing to cause a scene, grabbed his friend's arm to lead him away and continued walking. Just past the 24-hour copy shop and marital aids emporium, a man came up to try and sell them some watches. The suburban mouse thought one of the watches looked suspiciously familiar, but still they kept walking. Finally, on the street where he had parked his resource-guzzling, air-befouling automobile, he could find no trace of it.

"They . . . they towed away . . . " he stammered.

"Ah, fuhgetabouddit!"

Five floors up, in the city mouse's studio apartment, they capped their night off with a bit of Armagnac. The city mouse said, "See the excitement you're missing, living way out in the sticks where you do?"

"Oh, I do, I do," the suburban mouse said earnestly. "This has all really opened my eyes. Life here has so many possiblities! I can never thank you enough for such a wonderful night!"

"Ah, fuhgetabouddit!"

"No, really, this has been a groundbreaking evening," said the suburban mouse. "I feel so alive! It feels like life is a huge Broadway musical and I've got the chance to play the lead. This evening has allowed me to accept things I never have before. And I'm so grateful to you that I want you to be the first to know. I'm . . . I'm coming out of the wainscoting."

"You're what?" asked the city mouse.

"I'm attracted to other mice," he said.

"Well, it's a good thing, seeing as you're a mouse and everything."

"No," said the suburban mouse, "I'm talking about mice of my own gender."

After an infinitesimal pause, the city mouse exclaimed, "That's great! Thank you for sharing that with me. It's not exactly my piece of cheese, you understand, but I applaud your acceptance of who you are. If I can help in any way—help in a *general* sense, that is—don't hesitate to ask."

"Since you mention it," the suburban mouse said, "would you allow me to stay here with you until I can sell my baseboard in the suburbs?"

Although the city mouse didn't really have enough room in his place, what could he do but welcome his friend and lend him support as he embarked on his new life? Tempers flared a few times, such as when the city mouse scratched a couple of his friend's Judy Garland records, but things went smoothly overall. In a few months, the ex-suburban mouse found his own place downtown, as well as many new friends and interests. And every

Halloween the city mouse and the ex-suburban mouse got together for the big parade and celebrated another life saved from the shackles of monotonous middle-class conformity.